Trick-or-Treat!

To Diana Conway, thanks!
—A.D.

For Gina, Larry, Angie, Dominick, and Joseph
—L.D.

Text copyright © 1998 by Ann Dixon.
Illustrations copyright © 1998 by Larry Di Fiori.
All rights reserved. Published by Scholastic Inc.
SCHOLASTIC, CARTWHEEL BOOKS and the CARTWHEEL BOOKS logo
are trademarks and/or registered trademarks of Scholastic Inc.

ISBN 0-590-28161-5

10   9   8   7   6   5   4   3   2   1   8   9/9   0/0   01   02

Printed in the U.S.A.   24
First printing, September 1998

Trick-or-Treat!

by Ann Dixon
Illustrated by Larry Di Fiori

SCHOLASTIC INC.
New York   Toronto   London   Auckland   Sydney

Cartwheel
·B·O·O·K·S·®

One, two!
Two monster feet
tramping, stamping up the street.

Two worrisome, furrysome feet
searching for a Halloween treat.

Two more!
Two tyrannosaurus feet
thundering, blundering up the street.

Two plus two
makes four fearsome feet
looking for a Halloween treat.

Here come more!
Two ghoulish feet
creeping, crawling up the street.

Four plus two
makes six scary feet
walking this way for a Halloween treat.

Yikes! Two more!
Two pointy-toed feet
scuffling, shuffling up the street.

Six plus two
makes eight awful feet
coming closer and closer for a Halloween treat.

Not two more!
Two bony, groany feet
clinking, clanking up the street.

Eight plus two
makes ten terrible feet.
And I don't have one Halloween treat!

Please, no more!
Enough eerie feet
strutting, striding up the street.

What will I do?
Five horrible humans yell, "Trick-or-treat!"

"Boo!" I say. "Do you like *my* feet?"

At last, no more.
All ten feet
hurry, scurry down the street.

"May I come, too?
I'd like a sweet!"
"Hi, skeleton! Trick-or-treat!"

Two less.
Two bony, groany feet
scattering, clattering down the street.

Ten minus two
leaves eight afraid feet.
"Hi, witch! Trick-or-treat!"

Two less.
Two pointy-toed feet
fleeing, flying down the street.

Eight minus two
leaves six scared feet.
"Hi, ghoul! Trick-or-treat!"

Two less.
Two ghoulish feet
darting, dashing down the street.

Six minus two
leaves four frightened feet.
"Hi, tyrannosaurus! Trick-or-treat!"

Two less.
Two tyrannosaurus feet
hustling, bustling down the street.

Four minus two
leaves just two feet.
"Hi, monster! Trick-or-treat!"

Two less.
Two monster feet
racing, chasing down the street.

Two minus two
leaves zero feet.

Thanks for all the Halloween treats!

BOO!